One Mistake

by

Joanna Hines

First published in 2008 in Great Britain by
Barrington Stoke Ltd
18 Walker Street, Edinburgh, EH3 7LP

www.barringtonstoke.co.uk

ISBN: 978-1-84299-528-0

Printed in Great Britain by Bell & Bain Ltd

A Note from the Author

It's so easy to stick labels on people. And *good* and *bad*, *success* and *failure* are some of the labels we use the most. But people are always full of surprises – clever people act stupidly, people who seem boring turn out to have amazing secrets, and heroes are never what you'd expect. Just like Ben Sharp. In this book, nothing is how it seems. And that's how it is in real life. I've enjoyed getting to know Ben, his sister Emma and his girlfriend Karen, and I hope you enjoy meeting them too.

To Laura

Contents

1	Downhill	1
2	Charged	7
3	Emma	14
4	Blackmail	19
5	Max	23
6	Photos	28
7	Karen	33
8	Max's Bar	40
9	Rose and Ruby	46
10	The Price	50
11	Anya	53
12	Southern Comfort	60
13	The Row	66
14	Rupert	71
15	Trains	75
16	Show Down	79
17	Fire	85
18	No Escape	89
19	Away	95
20	Again!	99
21	Inside	108
22	Happy Couple	111
23	Hero	115

Chapter 1
Downhill

His dad's face had gone grey with pain.

"Ben," he said at last. "Why don't you drive us home? The hip's hurting a bit. You know how it is."

Ben stared back at his father in disbelief. The old guy was asking him to drive at last. Ben had thought the day would never come. So how was he meant to tell him that he couldn't do it?

"Go on, then, Ben," said his mum. She'd already started to open the car door so as to get into the back seat. "You're always saying how much you enjoy driving."

There was a warning prickle of sweat on the back on Ben's neck. A sure sign that things were about to go badly wrong. But it was only twelve miles from here to his parents' home. How could anything go wrong? He'd be OK, surely. No one could be that unlucky.

Could they?

"Right, Dad. No problem," he said. He opened the passenger door for his father, who sat down slowly. Ben saw the pain on his face. Poor old bloke, he'd been waiting months for the operation. Ben said, "I'll have you back home in no time."

"Thanks, Ben," said his dad.

His mum was settling herself on the back seat and clucking like a contented hen. She said, "I can't think why you threw in that delivery job you had. You were always going on about how much you enjoyed it."

"Seat belts on?" asked Ben. He fired up the engine.

It felt good to be behind the steering wheel again.

Three months had been far too long. Ben drove smoothly and well. Of course, it would have been better if he'd been driving a Ferrari or a Porsche, and not his parents' six-year-old Nissan in a yuck shade of green, but he wasn't complaining.

And it would have been much, much better if Karen had been sitting next to him in the passenger seat, to see how well he eased the car along through the traffic, instead of his dad, but still, he wasn't even complaining about that. It was good to be driving them home, helping them out a bit, showing them he wasn't all bad.

Ben was enjoying himself so much he didn't even mind when his mum and dad started talking about his sister's wedding. He knew they would. Emma's wedding was pretty much all they talked about these days. In two months his kid sister Emma was getting married. Of course, being Emma, the perfect daughter and all-round golden girl, she wasn't just getting hitched. Oh, no. She was going to have the wedding of the year because she was going to marry Rupert Coram. Golden boy. Rich, and on the way to being famous. Emma and Rupert were going to be the perfect couple, and no mistake.

It was enough to make Ben sick – only it didn't. He felt the same way about Emma that everyone else did and he was glad she was so happy. Anyway, why should he feel bad? He was on his way to see Karen again at last. Six weeks apart had been far too long.

"I wish I knew what Rupert's mother was going to wear," said his mum. And not for the first time. "I don't want us to clash."

His dad said, "Slow down, Ben. This isn't a race, you know."

"I'm inside the limit, Dad," said Ben.

"You're going too fast, I tell you."

Time was, that would have started an argument between them, but Ben was learning when to say nothing. He just eased his foot off the accelerator and thought about Karen. Her long brown hair and her smile that was kind and sexy and shy all at the same time. If all went according to plan, this evening was the moment when –

"Why is that police car behind us flashing his light?" asked his mum.

And his dad said, "I think he's telling us to pull over."

"Oh, dear. Oh, dear," said his mum. Starting to panic.

"Don't worry," said his father, as Ben pulled the car to a halt at the side of the road. "We're all legal."

Ben's good feelings had vanished. And he felt sick with dread. All legal, his dad had said.

That was what he thought.

All legal.

If only.

Chapter 2
Charged

Being arrested was worse than Ben expected. Much worse than when he'd lost his licence in the first place.

It was bad enough being taken back to the police station and waiting ages while he had his finger-prints and DNA swabs done. And then sitting for the mug shots. All that was grim. But the bit that really stuck like a knife in Ben's guts was remembering how shocked his parents had been. He couldn't get that picture out of his head.

"Why didn't you tell us you'd been banned?" his mum had wailed. She was so careful about everything. She even flew into a panic if they got a red reminder from the gas company to tell them they were late paying their bill. And now here she was standing on the edge of the road next to a patrol car with its blue light flashing. If anyone she knew had driven past at that moment, she'd probably have died of embarrassment right there.

"I didn't want to worry you," said Ben. Which was partly true.

"This is the last straw, Ben," his father said. "After all we've done. It's really the last straw. You're twenty-five, now. Time to grow up and act like a man."

Ben mumbled something that might have had the word "sorry" in it somewhere.

Worst of all was the way his father flinched as he eased back into the driving seat. Silent and uncomplaining as always, but you could tell it was torture for him to have to drive.

Ben tried not to think about it.

Sergeant Lewis, the red-faced joker who'd stopped them in the first place, had other ideas.

"Nice people, your folks," he said as they were driving back to the police station. Just in case Ben hadn't noticed it, obviously. "How'd they end up with a bad lot like you?"

"Luck of the draw?" Ben muttered.

"There's black sheep in every family," said Sergeant Lewis to the driver.

"Baa," said Ben. Not the most sparkling response, but the best he could think of just then.

"What was that?" asked Sergeant Lewis, his red face getting even redder.

"Nothing," said Ben.

At the police station there didn't seem to be all that much going on and Ben hoped it would all be over quickly. Sergeant Lewis had kept on about how he might be kept in the cells until the magistrates' court met in the morning, but Ben guessed he was only saying that to wind him up.

As a wind-up, it worked well. After all, he was due to see Karen in a couple of hours.

But then, just as he was being led to one of the holding cells for the police statement, there was a sudden noise and fuss. Phones started ringing and the whole sleepy Sunday afternoon feel of the place changed at once. As the holding cell door slammed shut behind him, Ben heard a police siren start up just below his window and move off down the road at speed, then a second one followed, then a third. The wailing of the sirens died away. Ben sat in the cell and listened to the heavy footsteps running up and down outside his door. What the hell was going on?

Ben had been in the cell for forty minutes, though it seemed like four hours, when the door opened and a police officer stepped in. He was young and looked more like a schoolboy than a cop. He had hair the colour of a ginger biscuit and Ben knew he'd seen him somewhere before.

"Hello, Ben," he said. He sounded friendly. "Long time no see. I just heard you got done. Sorry you've been kept waiting so long."

Ben looked at him. Why was he being so friendly? Ben waited for the "bad cop" to come in after him. Red-faced joker Lewis. "Do I know you from somewhere?" Ben asked at last.

"Yeah," said the officer. "A few years back. My first day at Stock Green. Some Year Nine psycho was starting to beat five kinds of shit out of me and you got him to back off."

"You sure that was me?"

The officer grinned. "Unless there's two Ben Sharps who live round here and went to

Stock Green. As I remember, you said you'd rearrange his face if he didn't leave me alone."

"I don't remember," said Ben.

"Well, I never forgot," said the officer. He held out his hand, "Ashley Carter," he said. "I'll make this as painless as I can. I owe you that much. Those bullies would've made my life hell if it hadn't been for you."

Ben shook his hand. He could hear an ambulance on the road outside, then another one.

"What's going on?" asked Ben.

"You haven't heard, have you?" said Ashley. "Someone found a woman's body in that patch of woodland past the BP garage."

"Suspicious?" asked Ben.

"Very suspicious," said Ashley. "She was killed with a blow to the head."

"It might have been an accident," said Ben.

"I suppose so," said Ashley. "But not many people crack their heads and then bury themselves in a pile of leaves. This one looks like murder."

Chapter 3
Emma

An hour later Ben was standing on the street outside the police station and thinking about what he should do now. He was due at Karen's in an hour and her place was nearly an hour's walk away. It would take him about forty minutes to walk home. At least then he could shower and put on some fresh clothes and bike it over to Karen's.

What does it matter anyway? he thought gloomily. Once Karen heard he'd driven while banned, there'd be no chance of them getting back together. He decided to go home first.

After all, if you're going to get dumped, you might as well scrub the finger-print ink off your hands first. At least he'd feel better about himself.

Ben had just walked to the end of the street and started to cross when a small white car screeched to a halt in front of him. He was about to swear at the driver for almost running him over when he saw who it was.

"Emma!" he exclaimed. "Good timing!"

His sister leaned over and opened the passenger door. "Jump in," she said. "I'll run you home."

"Thanks. Did Mum and Dad call you? That's good. Poor Mum was so shocked."

Emma shot through a red light. "I called them," she said. "I had to see you."

"Thanks," said Ben.

"I have to talk to you," said Emma.

"Yeah. Well. So long as we skip the lecture," said Ben. "Hey, what's your problem?"

Emma had steered suddenly to the left and almost clipped a Tesco lorry. "You shop, we drop," it said on the side. The way Emma was going, they were all going to drop before long.

"I'm in trouble," said Emma, and the car shot off fast again.

"Yeah. Well. So am I," said Ben. "But that doesn't mean I want to be wiped off the map. Jesus, Emma, watch out!"

Two teenage girls had stepped onto a zebra crossing. Emma whizzed over it, and they jumped backwards just in time.

What sort of trouble could ever bother Emma in her perfect little world? A spat with heart-throb Rupert, maybe. But then he looked at her. Emma was pretty. More than pretty, she was gorgeous – everyone agreed on that. She had a heart-shaped face, huge green eyes, a mouth like Julia Roberts and long fair hair.

People went all gooey round her because she was like some precious object that you have to handle carefully. She was so gentle and sweet.

But not today. Today she seemed to have turned into some kind of raving maniac. And there were two long scratch marks on her left arm. "What's up with your arm?" asked Ben. "You been fighting cats?"

Emma didn't even hear his question. "You have to help me, Ben," she sniffed as she crashed the gears. "I don't know what to do!"

"Well, slow down for a start," said Ben.

She pressed her foot down on the accelerator, clipped the edge of the kerb and bounced towards an oncoming bus. Ben put his hands on the dashboard. He noticed they were going past the woods where the murdered body had been found.

"Go easy," said Ben. "There's been a murder and this area's crawling with police."

Emma hadn't heard. She pulled out to overtake an old blue car. They were heading straight for a black 4 x 4.

Ben saw that her eyes were misted over and there were tears on her cheeks.

Christ, he thought, *I'm being driven by a deaf lunatic who can't even see!* And he was the one who wasn't legal. Sometimes it was hard to see where the justice was.

Chapter 4
Blackmail

If Ben needed any proof that Emma was in serious trouble, it was right there in the way she was driving. She'd always been such a careful girl, the kind who carried her milk in two hands so as not to spill a drop. And she was a good girl. Emma was the good one and Ben – well, Ben was not so good. That's how it goes in families.

At last she screeched to a halt in front of his flat. She yanked the hand-brake on so hard it almost broke off.

"What's up?" asked Ben.

"I'm in trouble," said Emma.

"Yeah. I kind of got that part," said Ben. "What kind of trouble? You've not been driving while banned, have you?"

"Of course not," she said, tossing her hair out of her eyes. "I'm not a total moron."

"Thanks." Ben let it go. "What then? Pregnant?"

"Don't be stupid," she said.

"So?"

Emma looked away. She kept fiddling with her engagement ring. It was huge, of course, and real. All flashing rubies and diamonds. No fakes for Rupert's girl. She lit up a cigarette, inhaled and mumbled her answer.

"What did you say?" asked Ben. "I didn't hear you."

Actually, he had heard her. He just hadn't believed what she'd said.

She gave a small cough, fiddled with her ring some more, then said again, "I'm being blackmailed."

"That's what I thought you said. Who by?"

She took another couple of puffs and fiddled with her ring. Then she said, "Max Stanley."

"Max Stanley!" Ben exploded. "What the fuck have you been doing with that tosser?"

Everyone round here knew Max Stanley. Everyone knew him. No one liked him. And no one in their right mind ever trusted him.

Max Stanley owned a bar in the dodgy end of town. Max's. It was the kind of place that seems cutting edge when you're about fifteen and which you get to know is just a dump by the time you're twenty. But Emma was twenty-two and about to get married to Rupert Golden-boy Coram. What the hell had she been doing with Max?

Maybe it wasn't as bad as she made out, thought Ben. After all, Emma was so innocent she probably thought the police would get her for not leaving a big enough tip or something.

But when she told Ben what had happened, he knew she really was in trouble this time. Big trouble.

Chapter 5
Max

Ben got Emma to tell her story again. It was just as bad the second time. If anything, it got worse.

Ben was trying to remember all he'd heard about Max Stanley. There had always been loads of rumours, but with Max, everything was rumour. People said the bar was only a front for a money-laundering scam. They said it was a cover for drugs. A place to get rid of stolen goods. Lately there'd been talk of prostitution. Girls from the Eastern bloc, mostly. Sex trafficking.

Lots of rumours, but for some reason, nothing ever stuck. Either the rumours were all lies, or else Max was too good at covering his tracks.

"Rupert went away for work last week-end," Emma had said. "I didn't have any plans, but I didn't want to stay in either. I thought I'd look in at Max's for a drink. Meet up with a friend and then go home. Have an early night. But then – I don't know how it happened. I got talking to Max. Well, I always knew he fancied me and he is kind of attractive, Ben."

"Only if you think rat-faced shits are attractive," said Ben.

"You don't understand," said Emma. "He's got something. Anyway, I was only talking."

"So what happened?"

"I must have been drinking more than I knew. Max kept giving me cocktails on the house."

"Did he spike your drink?" Ben asked.

Emma looked shocked. "I never thought of that."

Jesus, thought Ben. *How stupid can you be?* But that was Emma all over. She was really clever in some ways, but in other ways – well, a baby would have more sense. Ben had always had to watch out for her, just like she always stood by him when he was getting grief from their parents. They used to be a good team.

Of course, that changed when Rupert Coram turned up. Emma hadn't needed Ben any more. Until now.

"Go on," he said. A slow rage was beginning to burn inside him as she told the story again. "You went back to his place?"

"Yes." Emma's voice sounded flat and dead.

"And you had sex?" Ben asked.

"Yes. I suppose we must have done."

"You can't remember?" he asked.

Emma said, “I think so. But it’s all a bit muddled up in my mind.”

“You must have had sex with him if he says he’s got photos,” said Ben.

Emma started to cry again. Ben always hated to see her cry. She said, “You have to help me, Ben. If Rupert finds out, it will be the end of everything. My life’ll be over. I’d just die.”

“Oh come on, Emma,” said Ben, trying to stay cool. “It’s not that bad.”

“But it is,” she wailed. Really crying now. “I’ll lose Rupert and I’ll lose my job and I couldn’t live with myself. And all for one stupid mistake. Just one. You will help me, won’t you, Ben?”

“Yeah. Sure,” he told her. What else could he say?

“Thanks.” She gave him a teary smile. “I knew you’d help.”

"But I'm flat skint, Emma. How much does he want for the photos?"

She waited a moment. Then she said, "Max isn't interested in money. He says he's got plenty."

"So what does he want?"

"Me," said Emma. "He says all he wants is me."

Chapter 6
Photos

Ben was thinking to himself that something in Emma's story didn't add up. Max was the lowest of the low, but he just didn't see him blackmailing a girl for sex. Then he looked at the time.

"Shit," he said, "it's nearly seven. I'm due at Karen's in ten minutes."

"I thought it was over between you and Karen," said Emma.

"Yeah, it was. But we have this kind of fatal attraction for each other," said Ben. "I want to tell her we should try again." For a moment, he felt positive. But then he remembered how he'd spent his afternoon. His heart sank. He said, "Let's go inside. You can tell me what you want me to do while I get changed."

Emma locked up her car and followed him up the stairs to his flat. It was more of a room, really, but Ben liked to call it his flat.

She said, "You have to get the photos off Max."

"Yeah, I got that bit the first time." Ben took a clean shirt off a hanger. "Any ideas how?"

"I guess you'll have to break into his house." Emma made it sound like she was asking him to pick up an evening paper. "Then wipe the photos off his computer."

This struck Ben as an extremely bad idea, and he said so. "Maybe I'll talk to him," he said. "Try to make him see sense. The guy must see he's onto a loser. I mean, you're about to marry Rupert. No way are you going to dump him for a creep like Max Stanley."

"You don't understand," said Emma. "He's got a thing about me. He's obsessed. He's been obsessed with me for ages."

Ben thought she was making too much of it. Emma had always been a bit of a drama queen. He said, "Leave it to me, Emma. I'll go and see him tomorrow."

"No!" insisted Emma. "You have to go there tonight."

"But I told you, I'm seeing Karen tonight. It's been planned for ages."

Emma started to cry again. At least she wasn't driving now. "You don't get it, Ben!" she went on, "You have to destroy those pictures tonight, or Max will show them to Rupert tomorrow. Please, Ben. You're my only hope."

"But what will I tell Karen?" he asked. Not that it mattered all that much. Once Karen heard about his trouble with the police, he was history. So he might as well help Emma out.

Emma obviously thought so too. “You’ll think of something,” she said.

“Does Karen know about Max?” asked Ben. Emma and Karen had been friends for years. Emma had probably told her everything too.

Emma was so horrified she stopped crying. “No! And she must never know. Promise you won’t tell her, Ben.”

“OK. I promise,” Ben sighed.

“Thanks, Ben,” said Emma. “I knew I could rely on you.”

Suddenly Ben felt proud. Emma still needed him, just like she’d always done. He realised how much he’d missed his little sister since she got together with Rupert. Well, this was one thing that Rupert couldn’t help her with. But he could.

He said, "Leave it to me. I'll make sure Max never shows anyone those pictures."

"I'll give you his address," said Emma.

"Don't bother," said Ben. "I'll go to the bar first. He's there most evenings."

"What will you say to him?"

Ben grinned. "I'll think of something. And if he doesn't like what I say, then I'll wave my light sabre at him. Or else I'll just nuke the bastard."

Emma smiled for the first time that day. When they were kids they'd taken on all the forces of evil in their back garden. And beaten them, of course.

"Well, then," said Emma, "the guy doesn't stand a chance."

"That's right," said Ben.

He just wished he felt as confident as he sounded.

Chapter 7
Karen

Ben leaned his bike against the wall, snapped on the lock and rang the door bell.

Karen opened the door at once. She was looking great. You could see she'd taken a lot of trouble with how she looked and all for him. Her long brown hair was shining and she was wearing a tight black top that showed her perfect breasts.

"Karen," said Ben. There was a tight feeling in his chest. "It's good to see you again."

"You too," she said.

She stepped forward and he put his arms around her. It was supposed to be just a friendly kiss, a hi-and-it's-nice-meeting-you-again sort of kiss. But the moment he felt her warmth and softness in his arms, he couldn't help it. He put his lips on hers and kissed her properly. And she liked it. He knew she did.

"I've missed you," he said.

"And I've missed you, Ben."

God, it felt good to be holding her in his arms again.

Karen and Emma had been friends in school. Karen had had a bit of a crush on Ben, but back then he didn't think she was anything special. Then she went away to college and when she came back she'd morphed from ugly-duckling into swan. She was stunning.

Ben didn't waste any time. They started going together. Ben waited to get bored, like he always did with other girls, but instead it just got better. Karen had got her first job teaching at a primary school about half an hour's drive away and of course the kids thought she was great. And he was working for a delivery firm. They'd laughed a lot and told each other things they'd never said to anyone else. Oh, yes, and they'd had great sex too.

Until he lost his licence. Too many speeding offences and one case of drink-driving for good measure.

Which meant he lost his job.

He'd got depressed. Had no money. Maybe he'd even taken it out on her a bit. Whatever the reason, it wasn't long before she'd had enough.

Karen had dumped him.

He'd been surprised how much that had hurt. There'd been other girls in his life, but none of them came close to her.

A week ago he phoned her. "Karen, I get my licence back in three weeks. And I've got a job too. It's not much but it's keeping me going until I get my wheels back. Look, I'm sorry about what happened. Can we try again?"

And she'd said, "Yes".

So now here he was, holding her in his arms. He wished Emma hadn't made him promise to go and see Max Stanley that evening. For a moment, he even thought of forgetting about Emma, but he knew he couldn't. Not really.

Karen kept her arms round his waist. She said, "Did you hear the news? About that girl they found murdered? Scary, isn't it?"

"Scary for her, I guess," said Ben.

"I'm glad you're here," Karen murmured.

"Me too." He kissed her again, then said, "Karen, something's come up. I can't spend the whole evening with you. Not tonight, anyway. I wish I could, but –"

She drew away. "What's up, Ben?"

"It's Emma. She's asked me to help her with something."

"What?"

"Oh. You know. Just stuff."

Karen was staring at him and she wasn't smiling any more. Then she said, "Oh, by the way. I bumped into Tony last week. He said when you get your licence, you can have your old job back. That'll be a couple of weeks, won't it? You ought to go and see him."

"Yeah. I'll do that." Then Ben thought, *Why pretend? Karen will find out soon enough*, so he said, "No, I won't see him. There's no point."

"Why not?"

"I got stopped by the cops today. Driving while banned. I was trying to help my mum and dad. My dad's got this bad hip, you see, and it hurts him to drive. So he asked me to drive him home but it kind of backfired."

Karen folded her arms. The smile had died on her face and her eyes had gone cold and hard. She said, "Ben, tell me I didn't hear that. Tell me you didn't drive while you were banned."

"I did," said Ben.

"But there was only two weeks of the ban left!" said Karen. She'd been counting the days, too.

Ben said, "Well, it was a mistake. Obviously."

"You make too many mistakes, Ben. Why don't you just go?"

"We've got time for a drink," he said.

"No. I don't want to have a drink with you, Ben," she said.

"What about another evening, then?" he asked.

"No," she told him. She was angry, but it was the kind of angry that comes from being hurt, and Ben thought he still had a chance to put things right. She still cared for him. He was sure she did.

He said, "Look, Karen. I'm sorry about tonight. Blowing you out."

But she said, "It's not that. It's just that I thought you could change but now I see you never will. You're a loser, Ben, and I hate losers. My dad was a loser and my mum had to bring us up on her own. That's never going to happen to me."

"But Karen! You don't understand!" he said.

"Oh, yes, I do. Once a loser, always a loser. Get out of my life, Ben. And stay out! I don't ever want to see you again."

She went inside, and slammed the door in his face.

Chapter 8
Max's Bar

Max's Bar was crowded. There was the normal Sunday evening mix of school kids trying to look cool and people in jobs they hated getting ready for the week ahead by getting shit-faced. Ben didn't bother getting a drink. After all, this wasn't a social call. And he didn't want to get done for riding his bike while under the influence.

He spotted Max Stanley sitting with a couple of pals in low leather chairs at the side of the bar. He went over. "Max," he said. "I need to talk to you. In private."

Max looked up. He had dark hair and cruel eyes and skin like old porridge. There was an ugly scratch mark on his cheek, fresh and red. He looked every inch the lowlife. Ben decided Emma must have been crazy or blind or both at once to fancy him for more than a split second.

"Do I know you?" asked Max. As if Ben was just a piece of nothing.

"No, but you know my sister," said Ben. "Emma Sharp."

Max's cruel eyes flickered, like an alligator remembering yesterday's breakfast. He gave no other sign that the name meant anything to him. He said, "Yeah. I might know her. Didn't know she had a brother, though. Why's Emma's brother wasting my time?"

"My name is Ben." Max just looked at him. So Ben went on, "We need to talk."

Max was taking his time. To impress his two moronic side-kicks. At last he said, "Wait for me outside."

Ben's hands were fists in his pockets as he did what he was told. He was mad with anger at Emma. Right then, he blamed her that he'd lost Karen. He knew Karen would probably have dumped him anyway, once she found out he'd been caught driving. Even so, maybe if he'd been able to spend the evening with her ... And now here he was getting ordered about by Max Stanley.

He waited outside on the street for so long he was about to go back inside, when Max came out. He seemed surprised. "You still here?" he asked.

Ben kept his fists in his pockets and came right to the point. He said, "You've got something of Emma's that I want."

"Like what?" asked Max.

"Pictures."

"She told you about those?" Max sounded surprised.

"She told me everything."

"Did she now?" said Max. He looked at Ben properly for the first time.

"Look," said Ben. "I know you fancy her but it's a waste of time. We need those photos back. She's about to marry and she's crazy about her boyfriend. What happened with you was just a one-off. And it sounds like she didn't know what she was doing anyway."

Ben waited. Well, it was worth a try. He was counting on the fact that Max Stanley had thought Emma was an easy target, because she was so clueless. Once he saw she had a big brother who could look out for her, the man would back off. It had worked in the past.

Max was lighting a cigarette. He said, "A one-off with me. Is that what she told you?"

"Yeah. She told me about you being obsessed with her."

"She told you that?"

"Yeah," said Ben.

"Look," said Max. "Your sister might be a good-looking girl and I admit I've had my eye on her for a while, but I'm not the obsessive type. No way. I can get hold of a good-looking girl whenever I want."

"Bully for you," said Ben. "So what do you want? Money?"

"What I want is between me and Emma. It's not money and it's not her either."

"What then?" asked Ben. "I mean, snaps of you two having sex aren't going to make the front of *Hello!* are they?"

Max looked at him. "I'm beginning to ask myself just what that sister of yours did say. Are you sure she's your sister? You don't look much like each other."

"She's my sister all right. We don't look alike because I'm adopted," said Ben. "She came along later."

Suddenly, Max started walking towards a black BMW parked nearby.

"Get in, Ben. I want to show you something," he said.

"Where?" asked Ben.

"My place."

Chapter 9
Rose and Ruby

Max's house was a big, modern, footballers'-wives sort of pad on the edge of town. All sharp-edged brick and bright red flowers and huge windows. As they got out of the car, the silence was broken by the sound of a train rattling past. The railway line must pass along the bottom of his garden.

Max unlocked the front door and right away there was a pinging sound. He punched some numbers into the burglar alarm control panel, but Ben wasn't quick enough to see what they were.

Max led the way into the house. From out of the shadows came two dark shapes – pit bulls. Ben stayed by the door. These dogs didn't look the types to stop at a friendly lick.

Max stooped down. "Hello, Rose, hello, Ruby, old girl." He sounded almost human as he greeted his animals. He turned to Ben. "These are the only real women in my life. Aren't you, my beauties?"

Ben took a step forwards but Max held up a hand to stop him. "Careful," he said. "Don't try to touch them. They'll have your hand off soon as look at you."

Ben was back by the door in a flash. "Very friendly," he said. And this was the house Emma had asked him to break into! Thanks for nothing, Emma! He'd be dog-meat if he ever tried that.

Max said to the dogs, "Kitchen!" With a last look at Ben, as if they were sorry they couldn't enjoy a quick chew on his leg, the dogs padded to the back of the house.

"Go and sit down in there," Max said and opened the door to a large room with two enormous white sofas. "And stay where you are," he went on. "The girls can be a bit funny with snoopers. I won't be long."

Ben sat down on one of the sofas. He looked around. The room felt like it had had lots of money thrown at it but wasn't used much. It was cold, and a bit depressing. And Max Stanley and his guests must be pretty careless. The sofa was covered in reddish brown stains – wine, Ben guessed.

When Max came back he was carrying a lap-top. He put it down on a low glass table and pressed a key. A picture of a naked girl came up on the screen. Then another. *Emma.* "Enjoy the show," he said.

Ben felt sick. He wanted to protect his sister. He didn't want to see pictures of her naked, screwing this weirdo guy with his psycho dogs and his empty house. No way.

"No" Ben said coldly. "I'm not a fucking pervert."

"Watch," insisted Max.

Ben didn't move.

Max picked up the lap-top and shoved it right in front of Ben's face. So then Ben had to look.

A chill of shock ran right through him.

It was Emma all right. But she didn't look drugged and she didn't look out of it. She looked as if she was having the time of her life.

Having sex, yes.

But not with Max Stanley. Ben almost wished it was him.

Emma's partner in this bedroom romp was another woman.

Chapter 10
The Price

Ben was stunned. He didn't want to look at the photos flashing by on the screen, but he couldn't take his eyes off them. He couldn't believe that was his kid sister doing all that weird stuff. He'd known her all her life. He thought he knew her better than anyone else on the planet. Now he wasn't sure if he knew her at all.

The silence was shattered by the sound of a train speeding past. It sounded like it was only a few yards away. Then silence again.

Max handed him a drink – straight vodka. Ben knocked it back. He needed it.

The other girl in the photos had short dark hair and one of those foxy little faces, all pointy nose and chin and small white teeth. It looked as if she was making most of the running, but it was clear that Emma was enjoying herself too. There was just one of the pictures where Emma looked surprised, shocked. Even a bit scared. The last one. Then they went back to the beginning.

Max watched Ben closely. "These turn you on, don't they?" he said.

"No," said Ben quickly. Too quickly. They turned him on all right, but there was no way he'd admit that to Max. Or anyone else.

Max just laughed. "So, what do you think of your perfect little sister now?"

Ben didn't answer.

"No one forced her," said Max. "You can see that, can't you?"

"Did she know you were taking the pictures?" asked Ben.

This time it was Max who didn't answer.

Ben said, "How much do you want for them?"

"I told you," said Max. "It's not money I'm after and it's not her either."

"What, then?" asked Ben.

"You'll have to ask her that," said Max. "And then you have to make her see sense and play this my way. I can see you're a clever lad. I'm sure you'll talk her round. Because your sister's not been honest with you, Ben. Not honest at all."

Chapter 11
Anya

"Why the hell did you lie to me?" demanded Ben as soon as Emma picked him up. He'd walked away from Max's house and called her on his mobile.

"I didn't lie to you," she said. "I just told you Max was blackmailing me with photos. You're the one who assumed they were of him and me."

Ben tried to think back and remember if this was true. He wasn't sure. It might have been. He still felt angry. He said, "I never knew you fancied women."

"I don't. Not really."

"Then why did you do it?" asked Ben.

Emma said, "I don't know."

"We have to talk," said Ben.

Emma nodded.

They drove in silence the rest of the way to his place. Ben felt angry and embarrassed. He kept looking at Emma while she drove. She looked just the same as she'd always looked – apart from being tense and pale. But in some ways she seemed like a stranger.

He put on his seat belt. He thought he was in for more of her wild driving from the afternoon. But she seemed to have gone to the other extreme. She barely got out of second gear the whole time. It was as if she was in some kind of a dream.

A nightmare, more like, Ben thought.

"Now," he said, when they had gone into his flat. "You'd better tell me what this is about."

Emma said, “Do you have anything to drink round here?”

Ben went to the kitchen area and looked to see what he had. There wasn’t much. “This is all I’ve got,” he said, bringing a half-full bottle of Southern Comfort and two glasses.

“Right now,” said Emma, “I could drink lighter fluid.”

When he had poured them each a drink, Ben asked again, “So tell me, Emma. Why the girl?”

“I don’t know,” she said. “I’ve asked myself a hundred times. Rupert had gone away for the week-end, and I was on my own and I went to Max’s.”

“But you’ve got loads of friends,” said Ben. It was true. His sister was Miss Popular. Always had been.

“I know, I know,” she said. “But sometimes I feel so – it’s hard to explain, Ben. But I feel trapped.”

"Trapped?" That was the last thing Ben had been expecting.

"Yes, trapped. As if I can't breathe. I'm suffocating."

"But that makes no sense," protested Ben. "You've got everything. You've always done well at everything you tried to do. Everyone thinks you're amazing. You've got a fantastic job. You go on three holidays a year. You're going to marry a man who's crazy about you. You're buying a house together."

"Yeah, I know," said Emma. She sounded sadder than ever. "And in time we'll have a couple of kids and move into a bigger house and – oh, Ben! Can't you understand? It's all so fucking predictable and safe!"

Ben stared at her. For a moment he thought she must be winding him up. He said, "No, I don't get it. If you're getting cold feet, you don't have to marry him."

"But I love him!" she wailed. "He's everything I've always wanted."

"So what's your problem?"

"I don't know," she said. "I just wanted to try something different. Pretend I was a different sort of person. Just for one night."

"So you go back to Max's place and he finds you a woman to have sex with?" asked Ben.

"Well, I didn't plan it," she said.

"But that's what happened?"

"Something like that," she said.

"Did you know he was taking photos?" he asked.

"Of course not!" she said. "As soon as I saw he had a camera, I stopped right away. I tried to get the camera off him but he wasn't having any of it."

Ben looked again at the scratch marks on her forearm. He said, "Did you fight with him?"

"We had an argument," said Emma.

Ben was silent for a bit. He was trying to absorb this new Emma, a girl who wasn't as happy in her perfect life as he'd always thought.

"Fuck," he said at last. "I wish I knew what the hell was going on. Max says he doesn't want money and he doesn't want you. So what does he want? Why is he doing this?"

"He wants me to lie for him," she said.

"Why?"

Emma said, "He wants an alibi."

"A what?" asked Ben. For the second time that night he'd heard what she said but couldn't take it in.

"An alibi. He wants me to say that he was with me, at my flat, all of last week-end while Rupert was away."

"Were you with him?" asked Ben.

“Only that evening at his place. Not the whole week-end,” she said.

“So why does he want an alibi?”

Emma didn’t answer right away. She closed her eyes. She looked like she was about to throw up.

She opened her eyes and reached for the bottle. Poured herself another slug of Southern Comfort. Then she said, “I didn’t understand myself until this afternoon. But now I do. Now it all makes perfect sense. You know that body they found in the wood?”

“Yeah,” said Ben. Suddenly he didn’t want to hear what she was going to say next.

“That’s her,” said Emma. “Anya. The girl in the photos.”

“Fuck,” said Ben. “It can’t be.”

Emma nodded. “It is. And now she’s dead.”

Chapter 12
Southern Comfort

They had more glasses of Southern Comfort. Emma's story came out. Bit by bit.

Last week-end, Rupert had gone to Spain for work. Which left Emma on her own and feeling bored. That part of her story was still the same as she'd told it the first time.

Emma had had no special plan in her mind when she went to Max's bar. She said she felt restless, she wanted to do something different. None of her friends were there. She got talking to Max. He bought her drinks and asked her back to his place. Anya was there and before Emma knew what was going on, it was Anya who was kissing her, not him. Emma had been shocked, but also excited. She didn't fancy Anya, but she loved the idea of doing something so totally different.

Or, at least, that's what she was telling Ben.

Always, before, Ben had believed every word Emma said. After all, the perfect sister wasn't going to lie, was she? But now he wasn't so sure.

As soon as Emma saw Max was taking photos of them, the sex stopped. She'd been shocked and upset. That must have been the photo where she was suddenly looking like a frightened little girl. Max wouldn't give her the camera, but he agreed to put it away.

Max started coming on strong at that point. He told her that he'd fancied her for ages, that *she* was the girl he really wanted. He said no one else mattered.

He seemed to forget about Anya, even though she was still there, listening to every word. Was he using Emma to give Anya the push? Maybe. Anyway, Anya did not like what she heard. First she cried. And when that didn't work, she got angry.

She went for Max. Screaming and scratching, she attacked him.

"Is that how he got the scratch mark on his face?" asked Ben.

Emma nodded. "The girl had nails like knives."

Ben looked at two long marks on Emma's arm. "And that was Anya too?" he asked.

"I must have got in the way," said Emma, "and she lashed out at me."

"Then what happened?" asked Ben.

What happened next was that Max hit Anya. Just to defend himself, Emma said.

Anya fell and her head banged against the corner of a table. She was knocked out.

At least, that's what Emma thought happened. She'd been pretty upset by that time. After a bit Anya came round. She seemed to be OK again. Once Emma thought Anya was all right, she wanted to go home and Max drove her. Emma went to bed and when she woke the next day she almost thought she had dreamed the whole thing.

Until Max phoned her that afternoon. He said if anyone asked her, she had to say that he'd spent the whole week-end with her. Or else he'd show the photos to Rupert Coram. And he'd enjoy it. Or maybe he'd post them on the internet so the whole world could see what Emma got up to in her spare time.

"Did he say why he wanted you to lie for him?" asked Ben.

"He said the police might come asking questions. He said when he got back from taking me home Anya had gone. He didn't know where, but he thought there might be trouble."

"He didn't tell you he'd killed her?" asked Ben.

Emma looked shocked. "Anya's death was an accident," she said. "I saw what happened."

"You didn't see what happened after he went back to his place."

"I think when he got back he found she'd died. The blow to her head was a lot worse than he thought. Concussion happens like that sometimes. Then he panicked. That's why he tried to hide her body."

"I can't believe you're still trying to defend him," said Ben. "Have you forgotten all those stories about Max beating up women who pissed him off? I think what happened was that when he got back to his place Anya was still mad at him and they had another fight. And this time Max killed her. That's the reason he tried to hide her body and that's why he wants you to lie for him."

Emma was trembling. She said, "Max never meant to hurt her. I know he didn't."

"You know nothing about him," said Ben. "Just try telling the police that Anya's death was an accident. They've started a murder investigation."

Chapter 13
The Row

They had a blazing row, then. The worst of their lives.

Emma yelled at Ben. Then she cried. Then she yelled some more. She told him that if he wouldn't help her then her life was just about over. She might as well die.

Ben had never seen her like this before. So crazy and out of control. But no matter what she said, he stuck to his guns. There was no way he could let her help get a murderer off.

It wasn't just wrong – it was stupid. Ben knew Max wouldn't stop with that. If he did blackmail her with the photos now, then she'd be in his power forever.

Of course, Emma didn't see it that way. All she could see was that if Ben didn't help her, she was going to lose everything. The idea that her life would be turned upside down seemed to have made her part company with her common sense. She just couldn't see that Ben was right.

Ben was furious with her, but he stayed calm. Not only was she acting like a total moron, but he'd given up his precious evening with Karen just to have her yell at him.

All the same, Ben hated not being able to give her what she was asking. Not because she called him a coward and a wimp and told him he didn't love her enough to help her. All that stuff hurt, of course. But what Ben hated was that Emma was so unhappy. His kid sister's heart was breaking and there was nothing he could do to help her.

In the end, she gave up.

"I'm going," she said. "I thought you were the one person I could trust, but I was wrong. Good-bye, Ben."

Ben tried to give her a hug, but her body was stiff and unfriendly. He asked himself if they'd ever be close again, like they used to be.

He said, "Promise you won't do anything stupid, OK?"

She shook her head – maybe that meant she wouldn't promise, or maybe it meant she wouldn't do anything stupid. Then she left.

When she'd gone, the little flat seemed very empty. Ben made himself a coffee and thought for a while. Then he phoned a mate and got the phone number of the policeman who'd been friendly that afternoon. Ashley Carter.

"Shit, man," said a bleary voice on the other end of the phone. "D'you know what time it is?"

"This is urgent, Ashley," said Ben. "That woman who was found dead. Anya Something or other. Is there any way her death might have been an accident?"

There was a low laugh at the other end of the phone. "Not unless she buried herself under some leaves by accident after she'd died."

"But what if she hit her head and then the person she was with panicked and tried to get rid of the body –"

"Hit her head?" asked Ashley. "What are you on about, Ben? The poor girl was murdered."

"Are you sure?" asked Ben.

"Why are you so interested in Anya?" asked Ashley.

"Just curious. I'd hate to think someone might get into trouble just because she had an accident and then they panicked."

"An accident?" said Ashley. "People don't stab themselves by accident, Ben. Not where I come from."

"Stabbed?" asked Ben. Suddenly he remembered those red-brown stains on Max's sofa. *Not wine,* he thought. *Not wine at all. Blood.*

Anya's blood.

"That's right," said Ashley. "She was stabbed three times. Right through the chest and throat. Shit, I don't think I should have told you that."

"Thanks," said Ben. "You're a real pal, Ashley. Now go back to sleep."

Chapter 14
Rupert

Ben phoned Emma's number. Rupert answered.

"Can I talk to Emma?" asked Ben. "It's urgent."

"She's not here," said Rupert. "I was going to call you."

"What do you mean, she's not there?" asked Ben. "She left here an hour ago."

"I'm worried, Ben," said Rupert. He sounded almost human for once. "She's been acting so odd the last few days. Something's on her mind and she keeps telling me it's nothing. Do you know what it is?"

"Yeah. Sort of," said Ben.

"What is it, Ben?" asked Rupert. "Is she getting cold feet about the wedding?"

"No. It's nothing like that," said Ben. "Emma's crazy about you."

"Thank God," said Rupert. "I was afraid she'd stopped loving me or something. And that girl is everything I've ever wanted."

"Yeah, well. No worries there," Ben muttered.

"So what is it, Ben?" Rupert asked. "Is she in trouble?"

"You could say that," said Ben.

"What kind of trouble? Why won't she talk to me about it? She knows I'd do anything for her. Anything at all."

The poor guy sounded so sad and worried that Ben felt sorry for him. Which was ironic, when you thought about it, since Rupert was the man who had everything. Not the kind of person you normally bothered to feel sorry for. Ben hadn't known before how he felt about Rupert. He hadn't liked him much. But he'd just been jealous of him. And they were talking to each other for the first time ever.

Ben said, "She loves you, Rupert."

"Oh, God, I'm so worried about her," said Rupert. "She called me just an hour ago. She sounded so upset."

"That must have been just after she left here," said Ben.

"She wasn't making sense," said Rupert. "She kept telling me how much she loved me and saying she was sorry and she was crying. She said no matter what she did, I mustn't think badly of her. Then she hung up. When I tried to call her back, her phone was switched off."

Ben swore.

Rupert said, "I wish I knew what the hell was going on. Just before she hung up, she said 'good-bye' and it sounded so ... so final."

Ben was suddenly very cold. Emma had been saying "Good-bye"?

The same thought must have been going through Rupert's mind. He said, "Ben, Emma said 'good-bye' like it was – forever."

"Jesus," said Ben.

"You have to tell me what's going on!"

"I wish I could," said Ben. "Honest, I do. But I can't."

"Why the hell not?" asked Rupert, getting angry.

Ben said, "Because Emma's the only person who can do that."

He just hoped she'd still be around to do it.

Chapter 15
Trains

Ben tried Emma's mobile. Rupert said he'd been trying it all evening but it was still worth a go. Of course, it was switched off.

He was furious with himself. He should never have let Emma go, when she was in such a state. She'd kept saying her life was over. What did that mean? Was she planning to end it all? Or what?

And why had he waited till after she'd gone before he phoned Ashley? If Emma had known that Anya was murdered, that there was no way her death was an accident, then she'd have changed her mind about covering up for Max, photos or no photos. Maybe Emma wasn't thinking straight right now, but she wasn't totally stupid.

The phone rang. Emma! He answered it before the second ring.

It was Karen.

Ben had never thought he'd mind Karen phoning him. But right now, Emma was the only person he wanted to hear.

He said, "Karen, is Emma with you?"

"No," said Karen. "But she rang just five minutes ago. Ben, she sounded so weird, not like her at all. She wasn't making sense. She kept saying I had to understand her. That she had to do something and it was for the best and I mustn't judge her by what she did. She kept saying I must remember our friendship and all the good times. She was crying."

"Did she say where she was?"

"No," said Karen. "She wouldn't tell me anything. What's happening to her? I know you said you had to be with her this evening, so you must know. She sounded terrible."

"Yeah," said Ben. "She is kind of upset."

"Why?"

"You'll have to ask her that," said Ben. He was beginning to sound like a recorded message.

"What if it's too late?" asked Karen.

Ben didn't want to think of that. He said, "Are you sure she didn't say where she was? Give you any clues? Think, Karen. There must be something."

"No," said Karen. "I was just trying to make sense of what she was saying. She wouldn't tell me where she was. And I missed some of what she said because a train was going past."

"A train?"

"Yes," said Karen. "You don't think she's planning to throw herself in front of a train, do you?"

A train. Max's, thought Ben. The railway went right past the end of his garden. *Emma's gone to Max's. On her own.*

"I've got to go," said Ben.

"I'm calling the police," said Karen.

"Do what you want," said Ben. And hung up.

Chapter 16
Show Down

Emma's white car was parked on the gravel outside Max's house. For a moment, Ben was glad. At least she hadn't gone somewhere to end it all. But the good feeling didn't last long. It was gone three in the morning and Emma was alone with Max Stanley. The man who had murdered Anya and then dumped her body in some woods five miles away.

Did Emma know she was dealing with a killer?

Ben walked silently over the gravel. He kept looking all around him, listening for the friendly snuffle of the dogs. Emma had said they were locked in the house at night. He hoped she was right.

There were lights on downstairs and the curtains were open. Ben bent right over as he went near the house. He could hear voices – Max's and Emma's. They were arguing.

Ben kept in the shadows, but he lifted his head and peered in through the window.

Max was sitting on one of the enormous sofas. He had his back to the window. Ben could see the back of his head, and his hand holding a glass.

Emma was sitting opposite. She looked like she was about to do a runner. She was sitting on the very edge of her seat, holding her bag. She hadn't even taken off her coat.

She looked like hell. There were dark shadows round her eyes and she was fiddling with her rings the way she always did when she was nervous. And she was crying.

"Please, Max," Ben heard her say. "You have to destroy those pictures. I'll tell the police you were with me all that week-end, I promise."

"Yeah, I believe you," said Max. "But I'll keep the photos for now. Always have some insurance, that's my belief."

"And when I've made my statement to the police, will you get rid of them then?"

"I might do," said Max. "But I'll still have copies. They're on my computer hard-drive. Call them souvenirs of a happy evening."

Ben had thought Emma was pale before, but she went chalk white now.

"Jesus," she said, her voice so low that Ben could hardly make out what she was saying, "Then I'll never be free of you."

"That's right, darling," said Max.

"Never," said Emma again.

"Don't look so sad," said Max. "Just think of all the fun times we'll have. You and I have always had something special, haven't we?"

"So I might as well go to the police," she said. "What have I got to lose?"

"What have you got to lose?" asked Max. "Fucking everything, darling, that's what. Because if you land me in the shit with the police, then I'll tell them you were there when Anya died. I could say it was you she was fighting with. Once they start looking they'll find traces of you on her body, won't they? Your DNA. They'll think you killed her. It would be my word against yours."

"No one would believe you," said Emma.

"Maybe. Maybe not," said Max. "But you'd hardly come out of it smelling of roses, would you, darling?"

Emma put her face in her hands.

Ben had a good look at the window. How did it open? He needed to know in case he had to get into the room in a hurry.

It was open a bit but there was no way he could reach inside to get the catch. He'd have to smash the glass. He crouched down again and felt around in the soft earth of the flower bed for a stone.

His hand brushed against something smooth and metal. It fell over and Ben could smell petrol.

"What was that?" Max said inside the house.

"I don't know," said Emma. And then Ben heard her say, "OK, Max. You win. I'll do it your way. Do you mind if I use your bathroom?"

"Be my guest," said Max.

It sounded like Max had got up and come to the window to look out. Ben curled up small under the bushes beside the window and prayed that Max would not see him.

He prayed too that Max would not smell the petrol.

Now Ben knew what the petrol was doing there. Emma wanted to burn the place down.

Jesus, he thought, *what a crazy plan.*

If Max didn't give her what she wanted, then she was going to burn the evidence!

Chapter 17
Fire

Ben stayed hidden in the darkness until he heard Emma come back into the room. Max moved away from the window.

"I'll be off now, then," Ben heard Emma say.

"What's the hurry?" asked Max. He sounded edgy.

"Well, it's late. I've got an early start tomorrow." She was trying to sound cool and casual, but it wasn't working.

"Stay for a bit," said Max.

"No, I'd best be off," said Emma.

"I said stay!" Max barked at her. This time, it was an order.

Ben stood up straight and looked through the window. He was just in time to see Max grab Emma by the arms.

"Let me go!" she shouted. "I'm leaving right now!"

"Like hell you are!" Max yelled in her face. "What's the hurry, all of a sudden?"

And then Ben saw him look up. Look towards the hall. At the same time, Ben saw a flickering light come from the upstairs window. Firelight that lit the gravel and the garden with a weird orange glow.

"What the fuck?" roared Max.

"Let me go!" Emma was screaming and struggling.

Max kept hold of her with his right hand, but his left hand made a fist and punched her hard on the side of the head. "You stupid bitch!" he shouted. "You stupid fucking bitch! What the hell are you playing at?"

He drew back his hand to punch her again, but Ben picked up the empty petrol can and smashed it on the window as hard as he could. The glass didn't break the first time, but the can made such a noise that Max let go of Emma and spun round. She slumped down on the floor.

The second time Ben smashed the petrol can on the window, the glass cracked and the third time it broke.

"Leave her alone!" Ben was yelling as he put his hand through the broken window. He opened it and scrambled inside.

Max had crossed the room to stop him. "Get the fuck out of here!" he ordered.

"My pleasure," said Ben. "But Emma comes too."

"No way," said Max.

And Max pulled a hand-gun out of his pocket and pointed it at Ben.

Chapter 18
No Escape

Smoke was pouring down the stairs. On the floor, Emma groaned. She tried to get up on one arm, then coughed and flopped down again.

Sweat was rolling down Max's face. He held the gun, pointing it at Ben, but he kept looking back towards the stairs.

Then he kicked Emma and said, "Get up! This is all your fault. Go up and get the lap-top. I'm not going without those pictures."

"You're crazy!" said Ben. "It's a bloody inferno up there. She'll be killed."

"Serves her bloody well right," said Max. He kicked Emma again. "Get up, bitch. Get up when I tell you!"

Emma cried out, but she was too weak to stand.

The smoke was getting worse. Max lost control. He reached down and grabbed Emma by the front of her sweater. "Get up when I tell you!" he shouted.

His anger made him strong. Max held Emma upright – her legs had given way.

"Leave her alone!" yelled Ben.

Max laughed and whacked Emma in the face with the gun. Ben leaped at him.

There was a loud bang as Max pulled the trigger on his gun. The shot would have got Ben full in the chest, but just in time Emma let out a cry and bashed her hand against Max's wrist. The bullet pinged into the wall somewhere over Ben's head.

Ben charged into Max. Both men were coughing and spluttering now, and it was getting hard to see, but Ben landed a heavy punch on Max's jaw. Max fell backwards onto the sofa.

Ben reached down and caught hold of Emma.

"Come on, Emma. Let's go," he shouted.

But she didn't seem to hear him. Her eyes were open, but they were huge and shocked and she didn't move. For a moment Ben thought she must be dead.

"Emma!" he yelled.

Through the corner of his eye, he could see Max struggling to get up. His face was twisted and purple with rage. And he still had the gun in his hand.

Ben grabbed Emma round the waist and threw her over his shoulder.

He started to go to the hall, to leave by the front door, but the smoke was too thick and beat him back. With Emma slumped over his shoulder he crossed back over to the window and pushed her out. Max fired the gun again, but the smoke was so thick now, he was having a hard time seeing where they were. Ben heard her grunt as she fell on the soft earth. Then he climbed out after her.

"Come on, Emma. Run!"

She just groaned. At least she was still alive. Ben put his arm around her and half carried her away from the house. He had to get her away before the whole place went up.

Turning back, he saw Max's face at the window.

"Where are you?" Max yelled. And fired two shots into the darkness.

"Quick," said Ben to Emma. "Your car."

Max was already starting to climb through the window into the garden. Emma's car was unlocked, thank God.

Suddenly, Ben heard the sound of dogs barking and howling. He'd just shoved Emma into the passenger seat and was about to get in, when he saw Max stop. He was half out of the window. Max turned and looked back into all the smoke.

"Ruby!" he yelled. "Rose! Don't worry, I'm coming for you."

"Don't be an idiot!" Ben yelled.

But it was too late.

Ben watched in horror as Max dropped back into the room and vanished into the clouds of smoke.

Ben started to run back towards the house. "Get out of there, you bloody fool!" he shouted. "Get out before it's too late!"

The barking changed. Max must have got to his dogs and let them out. The barks were loud now, as if the dogs were running free in the garden.

Thank God, thought Ben. *If the dogs are out, then Max must be too.*

But the next moment he heard a terrible scream. And then silence.

Chapter 19
Away

"Ben, hurry!"

Emma was calling him from the car.

Ben didn't know what to do. He wanted to go and make sure that Max was OK. But then he heard two sounds that made him change his mind. He heard the noise of the dogs, running round the side of the house and baying for his blood. And he heard the siren of a fire engine, coming this way.

He ran to the car and jumped in, pulling the door shut just in time. The dogs leaped up at the window, snarling and showing their long teeth. Ben slammed the car into reverse and wheeled around, changed back into first and sped out into the road. The dogs chased him for about fifty yards, then gave up.

When the car reached the end of the road, the first fire engine shot past them, racing towards Max's house. Then another one.

Ben pulled into the side of the road. "I'm going back," he said.

"Are you crazy?" Emma shouted.

"I've got to tell them about Max," said Ben.

"He's OK," said Emma. "The dogs got out, so he must have done too."

"Didn't you hear that scream?" asked Ben.

"What scream?" Emma wanted to know.

Had he just imagined it? So much had happened in the last twenty-four hours, it was hard to make sense of everything.

Emma said, "Ben, just take me home. Please."

"All right," said Ben. And started up the car again.

"You won't tell anyone what happened, will you?" she asked.

"No," said Ben. After all, what was the point? "I won't tell anyone."

"Promise?"

"I promise," said Ben.

"You were brilliant back there," said Emma. "God knows what would have happened if you hadn't shown up."

Ben thought of Anya's body, covered in stab wounds in a shallow grave under the leaves. That could have been Emma. Then he remembered how she'd knocked Max's arm when he'd tried to shoot Ben.

He said, "You haven't done so badly either. You probably saved my life, you know."

Emma sighed with relief. She said, "We're proper heroes, aren't we?"

“I guess so,” said Ben.

That was when he saw the flashing light behind them.

“Oh, shit,” he said.

Chapter 20
Again!

Sure enough, it was a police car. Sergeant Lewis, as ever. Doing the early shift.

"Well," said the sergeant. He acted surprised to see Ben get out of the car. "I thought it looked like you, but then I said to myself, no. No one is that stupid. Looks like I was wrong. You really are that stupid, aren't you Ben?"

"Please," said Emma. "It's not his fault, honestly. I can explain everything."

Ben said, "Shut it, Emma." And to the sergeant he said, "Don't listen to her. She's just a bit upset. Row with her boyfriend. You know how it is."

The sergeant looked pleased with himself. His face got even redder. He said, "You'll have to do better than that, my son. Driving while banned twice in one day. I reckon you're looking at six months at least."

"No!" yelled Emma. "You can't do that! I won't let you! When I tell him why you were driving ..."

But Ben ducked down inside the car and said, "Emma, don't say a word. I'll handle this, OK? It'll be all right. I promise."

"Go on then, tell me," said the sergeant, sarcastic as ever. "What's your excuse this time? Saving a young lady in distress? I don't think so, somehow."

"No," said Ben. "You're right. I was just being stupid. Same as always."

Emma let it go right then. But afterwards she kept on at Ben that she wanted to tell the police everything. She came to see him in the police cells in the morning. He hadn't got bail.

Emma looked like she'd lost about half a stone. "Worry and lack of sleep," she said. She was very pale. But still as beautiful as ever.

Emma told Ben how Max's house was burned to the ground. Nothing was left – no sofas, no lap-top, nothing.

Ben waited till he was sure no one could hear what they were saying, then he asked, "Do you know what happened to Max? Did he get out OK?"

"No." Emma was shaking. She said, "They found his body just inside his kitchen. They say he died from all the smoke."

"He died saving those bloody dogs," said Ben. "I can't believe it. Why would anyone risk their life for a couple of dogs?"

"They were everything to him," said Emma. Then she said, "Ben, I can't sleep for thinking about what happened. I had to destroy those pictures. It was all I could think about – and then Max died. It's all my fault."

"He could have got out," said Ben.

"It haunts me," said Emma. "It will always haunt me. I can't believe I was so stupid. Everything that happened, just because of one stupid mistake. And now you're banged up in here."

"Well, it's not so bad."

"Ben, I can't let you do this," she said. "I can't let you carry the can for what I did. It's not fair."

He couldn't argue with her on that one.

"Then let me make a statement," she said. "If I tell them everything, all of it, then you'll get off without a prison sentence, I know you will."

"Everything?" asked Ben. "You'd really tell them everything?"

Emma swallowed. "Yes, Ben. I'd tell them everything."

"What? Are you crazy?" he asked, "You'd tell them about Anya and the photos and torching Max's place?"

"Yes," she said, so softly that he could only just make out the words, but Ben knew she meant it. "I'd tell them all of it."

"But that's crazy," said Ben. "That's arson. They'd throw the book at you. I'm looking at six months, tops. You'd get years."

"So?" she asked as if there was no hope.

"What about Rupert? What about your wedding and all your plans?"

"I know," Emma said, hugging herself. "But I can't live with myself. You're taking the rap for my stupid mistakes. What you did was brilliant. God knows what would have happened if you hadn't shown up at Max's when you did. You deserve a bloody medal.

And instead you're being treated like a criminal. It's all wrong."

Ben was tempted. He was sick of everyone thinking he was just nothing. His mum and dad had been to visit him, but you could tell they were dying of shame and couldn't wait to get out of the place. Not that he blamed them.

And the worst part of all was knowing that he'd lost Karen. Really lost her. She'd dumped him already for driving when banned. What kind of moron does that twice in one day? She must think he was the biggest loser on the planet.

If Emma went public with the truth, then Karen would know that he wasn't such a no-hoper after all. But he knew he couldn't let Emma do that. Not now.

He said, "Think, Emma. Max is dead. Nothing you do is going to bring him back. And he was a killer. Anya wasn't the first girl he'd got rid of. I talked to Ashley – he's one of the local cops – and he says a couple of other girls who'd been working for Max went missing too. The police had been onto him for months, just couldn't pin it. OK, so what you did was wrong, but if you go to prison and wreck your life, that won't make it better, believe me. Promise me you won't do anything stupid."

It was the longest speech he'd ever made to his kid sister. And it was worth it, just to see the look in her eyes.

"But it's not fair!" she said. Even so, Ben could tell that she would do what he said.

"Nothing's ever fair," he said. "We all know that. Cheer up, Emma. It's not so bad in here and it's not for long. The worst part of it is the fact that I'll probably miss your wedding."

"Don't be daft," said Emma, smiling for what seemed like the first time in ages. "And anyway, the wedding's cancelled."

"Cancelled? You didn't tell Rupert, did you?" Ben asked.

"Yes," said Emma. "Anya, Max, the fire, everything."

"Christ," Ben was amazed. "No wonder he broke it off."

"Not him," said Emma. "I did. I couldn't go through with it."

"Now you've lost me," said Ben. "This just doesn't add up."

Suddenly Emma was crying. She said, "He was so great about it. Of course, he was shocked and upset, but then he said he understood. And oh, Ben, that made me feel so terrible. I wanted him to be angry and shout at least, but he just said he loved me same as always."

"Well, maybe he does," said Ben. He remembered how worried Rupert had sounded when they talked the other night. He was beginning to change his opinion of Rupert Coram.

"But I can't stand it," said Emma. "I've screwed up badly and messed up people's lives and everyone is being so fucking nice about it! It's driving me crazy!"

Ben grinned. "Don't worry," he said. "I'll find a way to make us even."

"I'll hold you to that," said Emma.

Chapter 21
Inside

Inside, Ben had plenty of time to think.

He thought about Karen, and missed her. It hurt. Karen must have given up on him now.

He thought about Emma, and how he'd always thought she couldn't put a foot wrong. The apple of his parents' eyes. He tried to work out why she'd ever gone back to Max's house in the first place. Why had she let herself get involved in that girl-on-girl action with Anya? Maybe it was the way she said – she'd just gone crazy for a bit.

Then he thought about how she'd wanted to go to the police and tell them the truth, even though it would mean the end of all her hopes for the future. And he thought, not many people would do that for you. It took a special kind of person, so what did it matter if she'd made a stupid mistake, just once in her life?

He thought about Rupert Coram. He remembered how cut-up the guy had sounded when Ben spoke to him the night Emma went missing. And he thought how much it must have hurt him to learn what Emma had done that week-end he was away. Ben could imagine what he'd felt like. He knew how he'd feel if Karen had told him a thing like that. Would he have been able to forgive her? Of course he would. No doubt about it. Just like Rupert and Emma.

The wedding was back on again. One time when Emma came to see him after about six weeks, the ring was back on her finger. She said everything that had happened had brought them closer than ever. Lucky them. Ben couldn't help feeling jealous.

But most of all, Ben thought about Max Stanley. The man was about as evil as a man could be. He'd killed Anya, and probably those other girls as well. And now that he was dead, all sorts of stories were coming out about him. Worse even than the ones Ben had heard before. Max kept girls locked up. Beat them and raped them. Sold them on. Some of them were just kids. He was as bad as it got.

And yet, Max died because he went back into the burning house to save his precious dogs.

Ben thought about that, a lot.

Chapter 22
Happy Couple

Ben stood at the side of the room. He didn't want to be there. The wedding had been at their local church and Emma looked like she'd just stepped down off the top of a Christmas tree, so pretty in her dress of cream lace. Ben sat next to his mum and dad in the front pew and his mum cried. But when Ben put his hand on her arm, she stiffened and pulled away.

He was an embarrassment to them – their son, Ben, who'd gone to the bad. The boy with the criminal record.

Now the wedding party was in the Royal Hotel, and Emma and Rupert were greeting their guests and everyone was drinking champagne and talking and laughing.

Which was fine, but right now, Emma and Rupert were the only two people in the room who weren't making Ben feel like he was a bad smell. Emma had hugged him for ages and cried, and Rupert put his arms round him and said how glad he was that Ben was there. You could tell he meant it. But everyone else treated him like a leper.

There was no sign of Karen. Which was just as well. Ben didn't think he could stand to be in the same room with her. He knew he'd blown his chances with her forever. She probably wouldn't even want to talk to him.

She must have stayed away just because she didn't want to see him. No way would she have missed the wedding otherwise. Karen and Emma had been good friends from way back.

Ben tried to tell himself that he didn't mind. But that was all crap, because he did mind. He minded like hell.

His Uncle Ray came up to him and started going on about what a lovely bride Emma was. And how it made him remember his own wedding day, which made him sad because his wife Susan had died two years ago and he wasn't over it yet. And then he started on about his little dog and how lonely he was.

"Yeah," said Ben from time to time. And, "That's sad," because you had to feel sorry for the old guy. And it was nice of Uncle Ray to talk to him, because no one else would. But after a bit, Ben began to think he'd been better off standing on his own.

And then he saw Karen.

She was wearing a pale blue dress with those thin little straps that showed off her beautiful shoulders and she was kissing Emma and hugging Rupert.

Just seeing her made Ben sure. There was no way he could spend the whole evening in the same room with her. It was too hard to carry on as if he didn't mind not talking to her. Not being able to touch her.

He turned to go.

But just as he got to the door, he felt a tap on his shoulder.

"Ben? You're not going, are you?"

It was Karen.

Chapter 23
Hero

Ben looked down at her. She'd got some kind of sparkly stuff in her hair and she was looking fantastic.

He said, "Yeah, I'm off. I only got out last week. Not used to this kind of thing. All these people."

It was pathetic, but it was the best thing he could think of saying right then.

Karen nodded, as if what he said made perfect sense. "I never thought of that," she said. "Can I come with you? We can go somewhere else if you'd rather."

Ben stared at her. "Why?" he asked. "What's the point?"

"I want to talk to you," she said. "I want to say I'm sorry."

"What?" asked Ben.

Karen said softly, "Emma told me, Ben. She told me everything."

Ben felt as if someone had just punched him in the stomach. "She did?" he asked.

"Yes," she said.

"When?"

"This morning," said Karen. "When I was helping her get ready. She said you made her promise not to tell anyone. But she knew we'd both be at the wedding and she had to let me know. She couldn't keep on lying to me. So she told me."

Ben was having a hard time taking this in.

Karen said, "She told me about Max and that girl who got killed and the photos and the fire. Everything. And she said she wanted to go to the police and tell them what had happened, but you wouldn't let her."

"There wasn't any point," said Ben. "I'd still have been done for driving while banned, but Emma – well, God knows what would have happened to Emma."

"You've always protected her," said Karen. "She got away with murder when she was a kid, thanks to you." Then she put her hand over her mouth, as she thought about what she'd just said.

"Max died because of the dogs," Ben said. "He had plenty of time to get out."

"Emma's been an idiot. But you've always looked out for her. That's what I liked about you from the first."

Ben grinned. "You mean it wasn't my good looks and charm?"

"Oh, yes," she said. "That helped."

Ben said, "Why are you telling me this now, Karen?"

She said, "I wanted to come and see you while you were in prison, but I thought that I was just being weak. I was so afraid of being like my mum. I didn't want to end up with a loser. But now I know the truth."

"Are you saying we could maybe try again?" asked Ben.

"If you want," she said. "We could give it a try."

Ben looked all around the room, at Emma and Rupert and their families and their guests. Everyone getting pink and merry with the champagne. A moment ago, he'd felt like a leper. Now he felt like the luckiest man in the room.

He said, "But I'm still a loser, Karen. I've lost my licence and even if I get the old job back, it wasn't much. Everyone'll think you're crazy if you get hooked up with a bad lot like me."

"I don't care what they think," said Karen. "Because I know what they'll never know."

"And that is?" asked Ben.

"You're a hero, Ben Sharp. A real hero."

"Don't talk soft," said Ben. He smiled.

Want *more?*

Revenge

by

Eric Brown

**Dan's got everything –
and everything to lose.**

Dan Radford has it all. He's a pro footballer with a big house, fast cars – and a drink problem.

But the star striker is dragged into a nightmare of violence, kidnap, and blackmail. Dan has an enemy – and he's out for revenge.

You can order *Revenge* directly from our website at:
www.barringtonstoke.co.uk

Want *more?*

Sawbones

by

Stuart MacBride

They call him Sawbones: a serial killer touring America, kidnapping young women.

The FBI are trying to catch him – but they're getting nowhere.

The latest victim is Laura Jones: 16, blonde, pretty … and the daughter of one of New York's biggest gangsters.

Laura's dad wants revenge – and he knows just the guys to get it. This time, Sawbones has picked on the *wrong* family.